Since 1888, *National Geographic* magazine has provided its readers a wealth of information and helped us understand the world in which we live. Insightful articles, supported by gorgeous photography and impeccable research, bring the mission of the National Geographic Society front and center: to inspire people to care about the planet. The *Explore* series delivers National Geographic to you in the same spirit. Each of the books in this series presents the best articles on popular and relevant topics in an accessible format. In addition, each book highlights the work of National Geographic Explorers, photographers, and writers. Explore the world of *National Geographic.* You will be inspired.

T0306540

ON THE COVER
A pair of critically endangered red wolves
Photo by Joel Sartore

ENDANGERED SPECIES

Coquerel's sifaka,
a lemur native
to Madagascar

The world around you probably looks lush and healthy. The grass is green and thick in the summer, and you don't have to look far to spot a bird overhead or a squirrel running on top of a fence.

For some animals, though, the world has become an inhospitable place. Every day, Africa loses another precious rhino. Time is running out for the tiger and other big cats in the shrinking grasslands of Asia and Africa. The problem is both distant and nearby. In 2013, 2,054 species were listed as endangered or threatened. Of these, 1,436 were in the United States.

What puts so many species under such pressure? Disease, competition with other species, and natural hazards such as storms and fires all contribute. Humans play a big role, too. As human populations expand, we take over natural habitats, farming and paving over forests and wetlands. Hunting and fishing bring variety to our dinner tables but also deplete the numbers of some species. And the laws themselves often do little to protect species in crisis. There are many reasons to worry about threatened animals, even as we celebrate the stories of species that are making a comeback.

Part of the National Geographic Society's mission is to educate everyone about the amazing species that share our planet and to help protect them. The articles in this book—adapted from *National Geographic* magazine— shine the spotlight on various endangered animal species. Some, such as the polar bear, seem almost certainly doomed. Others are success stories, such as right whales and whooping cranes, which reached the brink of extinction and are now returning slowly. You'll meet scientists and conservationists who have dedicated their lives to preserving ecosystems and species.

Can the world of the future be a safer and richer place for all species? Read. Reflect. Be inspired to act.

PAINTED DOGS
Sometimes called "painted dogs," African wild dogs are native to sub-Saharan Africa. They are an endangered species because of shrinking habitats and diseases from domestic animals. This pair was photographed by Joel Sartore for his Photo Ark project.

ON THIN ICE

BY SUSAN McGRATH

Adapted from "Polar Bears on Thin Ice," by Susan McGrath, in *National Geographic*, July 2011

SHRINKING SPACE
A polar bear stands on a melting piece of floating ice on a summer evening in Manitoba, Canada.

THE ARCTIC IS warming fast. By 2050 it may be largely ice-free in summer. Without their frozen hunting platform, how will polar bears survive?

THEN AND NOW

In August 1881, naturalist John Muir was sailing off Alaska, searching for three ships that had gone missing in the Arctic. Off Point Barrow he spotted three polar bears, "magnificent fellows, fat and hearty, rejoicing in their strength out here in the icy wilderness."

If Muir were sailing off Point Barrow today, any polar bears he'd see would not be living in a wilderness of ice. They'd be swimming through open water, burning their precious fat reserves. That's because the bears' sea-ice **habitat** is disappearing, and it's going fast.

Polar bears live in the Arctic where air, ice, and water come together. Superbly adapted to this harsh environment, most spend their entire lives on the sea ice. They hunt year-round, visiting land only to build birthing dens. They prey mainly on ringed and bearded seals. Sometimes they catch walruses and even beluga whales.

Sea ice is the foundation of the Arctic marine environment. A surprising variety of organisms live underneath and within the ice itself. The ice is not solid but pierced with channels and tunnels large, small, and smaller. Trillions of tiny sea creatures pepper the ice. In spring, sunlight penetrates the ice. Algae begin to bloom. The algae then sink to the bottom, and in shallow areas they sustain a food web that includes clams, sea stars, arctic cod, seals, walruses—and polar bears.

Experts estimate the world's polar bear numbers at 20,000 to 25,000. Bears in the Norwegian islands, the Beaufort Sea, and Hudson Bay have been studied the longest. In western Hudson Bay, where ice melts in the summer and freezes back to shore in the fall, the creatures' predicament first came to light.

Ian Stirling, now retired from the Canadian Wildlife Service, has monitored polar bears in Canada since the late 1970s. He found that they **gorged** on seals in the spring and early summer, before the ice broke up. They then retreated to land as the ice melted. In a good year, when the ice started to break up, the bears had a thick layer of fat. Once on shore, the bears entered a state known as walking **hibernation**. Their **metabolisms** slowed down to hoard the fat stored in their bodies. "Until about the early 1990s at Hudson Bay," Stirling says, "bears were able to **fast** through the open-water season of summer and fall because hunting on the spring sea ice was so good."

During their years of bear watching, Stirling and his colleague Andrew Derocher began to notice an alarming pattern. They observed that the polar bears' population held steady, but the animals were getting thinner. The western Hudson Bay bears were missing weeks of peak seal hunting. In addition, the later winter freeze-up was extending their fasting time. By 1999 Stirling and Derocher had connected a steady decline in polar bear health with a decline in sea ice. Bears didn't grow as large, and some came ashore notably skinnier. Females gave birth less often and had fewer cubs. Fewer cubs survived. Within a few years, scientists in other parts of the Arctic began to see similar changes in sea ice and the polar bear populations.

The world didn't know it yet, but during the summer in the Arctic Ocean, sea ice had been melting earlier and faster. The winter freeze had been coming later. In the three decades since 1979 the extent of summer ice has declined by about 30 percent. The lengthening period of summer melt threatens to destroy the whole Arctic food web.

Data now support the early warning signs. Since Muir sailed in the waters off Alaska, the Earth has warmed about 1°F due in part to **greenhouse gases**. This may not seem like much, but even one degree of warming can disrupt an environment of ice and snow.

Bears
at Sea

The minimum extent, or range, of sea ice in summer has declined by about 30 percent since regular satellite monitoring began in 1979. Even in the winter the ice does not fully recover. In some areas, when females return in autumn to the sites where they make their dens, they face daunting expanses of open water. The Canadian high Arctic and northern Greenland could be the last refuges for polar bears, and even in these areas the ice will disappear if greenhouse gases are not reduced.

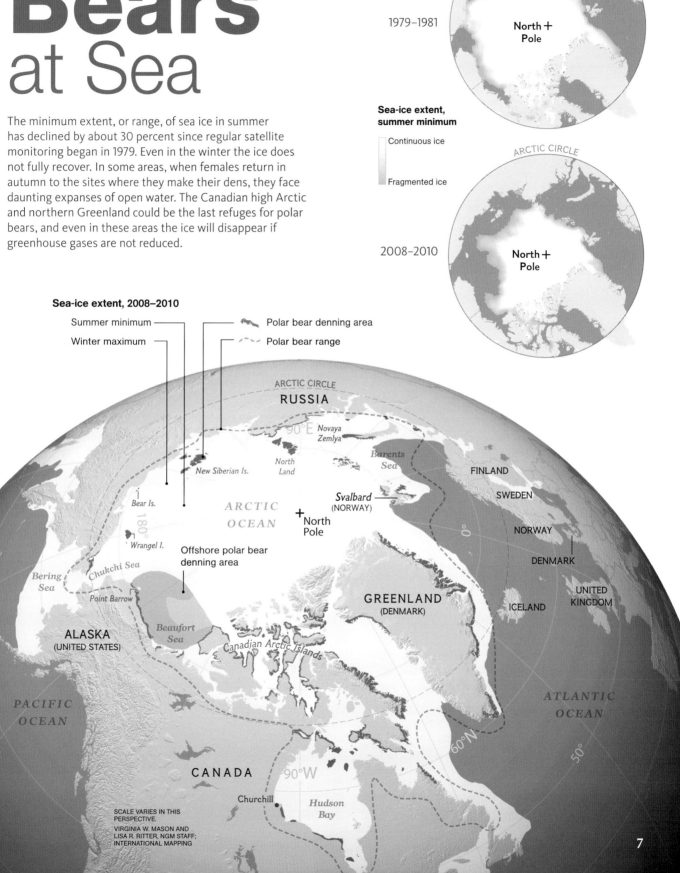

1979–1981

Sea-ice extent, summer minimum

Continuous ice

Fragmented ice

2008–2010

Sea-ice extent, 2008–2010

Summer minimum

Winter maximum

Polar bear denning area

Polar bear range

Offshore polar bear denning area

ARCTIC CIRCLE
RUSSIA
Novaya Zemlya
North Land
New Siberian Is.
Barents Sea
FINLAND
SWEDEN
Bear Is.
ARCTIC OCEAN
Svalbard (NORWAY)
NORWAY
Wrangel I.
North Pole
DENMARK
Bering Sea
Chukchi Sea
Point Barrow
Beaufort Sea
GREENLAND (DENMARK)
ICELAND
UNITED KINGDOM
ALASKA (UNITED STATES)
Canadian Arctic Islands
PACIFIC OCEAN
ATLANTIC OCEAN
CANADA
Churchill
Hudson Bay

SCALE VARIES IN THIS PERSPECTIVE.

VIRGINIA W. MASON AND LISA R. RITTER, NGM STAFF; INTERNATIONAL MAPPING

YOUNG FAMILY
A female polar bear leads her
cubs over floating ice in the
Svalbard Archipelago, Norway.

HARD TIMES

The sea ice above shallower waters provides the richest food source for polar bears. Recently, though, the ice has been retreating far from those areas. This retreat has reduced the length of the summer habitat bears need most to survive. Whether a polar bear lives in Hudson Bay or Barents Sea, it faces the same problem. Bears are forced to fast for longer periods because of less hunting time on sea ice. Also, thinner sea ice is more easily shifted by winds and currents. Bears may be swept into strange territory, where they must make longer, more difficult swims in open water to find favorable sea ice or get to land.

Polar bears are strong swimmers, but swimming long distances in open water can be fatal. In 2008 a radio-collared bear with a cub swam an astounding 427 miles to reach the ice off the northern Alaska coast. The cub didn't make it. In September 2004, researchers spotted four dead polar bears afloat after a storm in the Beaufort Sea. As many as 27 bears may have drowned in that one storm.

Females face especially hard times. Starving males kill and eat cubs—and the cubs' mothers. This behavior may become more common as food diminishes. Increasingly, getting to the places on land where the bears have made their dens for generations can be an ordeal. On one island, when the sea has frozen late in the year, scientists have seen few, if any, dens the following spring. According to Jon Aars of the Norwegian Polar Institute, they would normally see 20 or more dens. Whether females find other sites or skip a year of breeding, Aars can't say.

From childhood we create a picture of our physical world. The ocean is blue. The Arctic is white. But before this century ends—and perhaps much sooner—most of the Arctic will likely be blue water every summer. Can a blue Arctic support polar bears? Only in the short run, Stirling and others say.

Currents still cram drifting sea ice against the Canadian Arctic Islands and northern Greenland in summer. These pockets may hold enough ice to support polar bears through this century. But if the world keeps warming, not even those last refuges will be able to save the polar bear.

THINK ABOUT IT! ||||||||||||||||||||||||||||||||||||

1 **Summarize** In your own words, describe the impact of decreasing sea ice on the polar bear.

2 **Make Inferences** The article says that the polar bear stands at the top of the Arctic food web. What does this mean?

3 **Analyze Cause and Effect** What difference has 1°F of Earth's warming made in the Arctic?

POWERFUL SWIMMER
A polar bear swims toward land in the icy waters off Spitsbergen Island in Norway.

BACKGROUND & VOCABULARY

fast *v.* to eat no food

gorge *v.* (GORJ) to eat until completely full

greenhouse gases *n.* the gases in the atmosphere that trap heat and contribute to global warming

habitat *n.* (HAB-uh-tat) the environment where an animal naturally lives or once lived

hibernation *n.* (hy-bur-NAY-shuhn) a state of deep, long rest, especially through the winter

metabolism *n.* (muh-TAB-uh-lihz-uhm) the bodily processes involved in turning food into useful energy

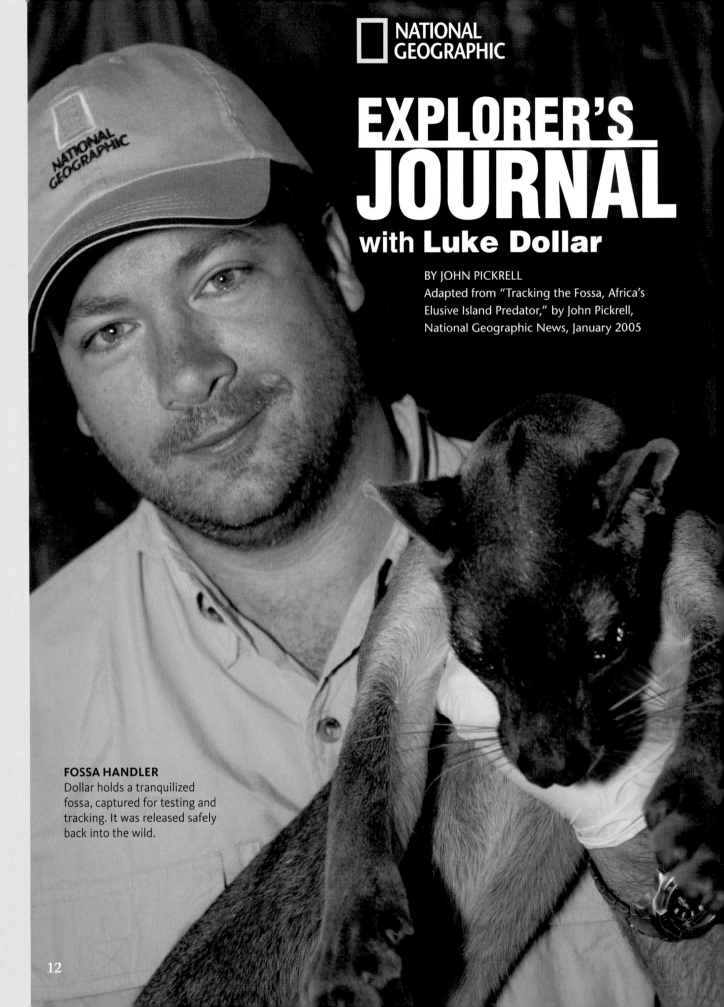

NATIONAL GEOGRAPHIC

EXPLORER'S JOURNAL

with **Luke Dollar**

BY JOHN PICKRELL
Adapted from "Tracking the Fossa, Africa's
Elusive Island Predator," by John Pickrell,
National Geographic News, January 2005

FOSSA HANDLER
Dollar holds a tranquilized
fossa, captured for testing and
tracking. It was released safely
back into the wild.

National Geographic Explorer and conservation scientist Luke Dollar works tirelessly on the island of Madagascar. His passion? Protecting a unique species and its precious habitat.

HOW IT ALL STARTED

After 20 years, Luke Dollar is still excited about his job. He says, "When you're in the field, it's muddy, sweaty, stinky, gritty, but it's great fun. I wake up every morning knowing I'm one of the luckiest guys on Earth because I'm doing exactly what I want to do and it's going to make a difference."

Dollar started his work in Madagascar as a student tracking lemurs. One day, one of the lemurs he was studying suddenly vanished from the rain forest. That event marked the beginning of a love affair with this mysterious predator. When Dollar finally found his missing lemur, all that remained were a few bones and tufts of fur. His guide believed that that the lemur had been eaten by a fossa.

Dollar was curious. Here was an animal that he and most other wildlife experts had never heard of. Two years later he returned and began a field project that would chart the secret life of the fossa for the first time.

The fossa was once mistaken for a primitive kind of cat. "Imagine a short, stocky mountain lion," Dollar describes. The fossa has several feline, or cat-like traits, including retractable claws and sharp teeth. Other fossa features hint at the animal's non-feline nature, including a snout like a dog's, a long tail used as a balancing pole, and the ability to "fly" through the trees like a squirrel.

In fact, the fossa is a close cousin of the mongoose and a member of the family that also includes meerkats and civets. Its scrappy temperament is also much like that of a mongoose. Also like its cousins, the fossa is an opportunistic hunter. It feeds on lemurs and on a wide range of animals, from mice to wild pigs.

Explorers first described the fossa in the 1800s. But even though it sits at the top of the food chain in one of the world's hot spots for biodiversity, researchers have very little information about the elusive animal. That could be due to the predator's amazing ability to conceal itself. In fact, until recently scientists assumed the fossa was nocturnal. Researchers now know it is diurnal, which means it is active during the day as well as at night.

Back in 1996, Dollar's first task was simply to confirm the presence of the secretive animal in those forests. One of his colleagues, Deborah Overdorff, had never caught sight of the beast, even though she had spent more than ten years working in fossa territory.

"Individual lemurs, under study for many years, would be there one day and gone the next," says Overdorff. The threat of predators helps determine whether primates such as lemurs will thrive in an area. The fossa is the lemur's most significant predator. By studying fossas, Dollar has been able to determine the threats that lemurs face.

A LOST WORLD

Many of Madagascar's creatures—including the fossa and more than 100 species of lemur—are found nowhere else on Earth. Madagascar is an island about twice the size of Arizona. It sits east of Mozambique in the Indian Ocean. The history of Madagascar helps to explain the unusual collection of the more than 200,000 plants and animals that live there.

"Madagascar has been called the eighth continent, and biologically speaking, that's a great name," says Stuart Pimm, a former member of National Geographic's Committee for Research and Exploration. "The species are not just varieties of African birds and plants but entirely new families," he said. "Madagascar really is a whole new world."

relative of today's fossa would have weighed more than twice as much as a modern fossa. It "could definitely have been seen as a threat by people," Dollar says. Not nearly as fierce as its reputation, the modern fossa presents little threat to humans. Even so, tales of long-gone giants might explain why the people who live in Madagascar today are often afraid of the fossa.

UNDERSTAND AND PROTECT

Since 1994, Dollar has perfected methods for capturing the animals with both cameras and wire cages. Trapping fossas gives the team a chance to give the animals a quick health checkup and put radio collars on them before releasing them back to the wild. Radio collars track how far fossas range (up to 16 miles per day). Genetic and scat analysis provide data on the fossa's diet. This information is used to better understand and protect the fossa, which is definitely at risk of extinction.

Just eight percent of the forest that existed before humans arrived on Madagascar remains today. Fewer than 3,000 fossas live in these undisturbed habitats. Also, new diseases, such as rabies, introduced to the island by pet dogs and wild cats, threaten the fossa. Dollar is also concerned about the threat that two new predators—a species of wild cat and the Indian civet—are posing to the fossa and other animals on the island.

Fossa research has led to development and ecotourism. These activities bring money into the poverty-stricken region for perhaps the first time. Many people in Madagascar make a living by farming just enough to live on. But now some are building new cabins in the park, which will provide the first permanent lodging for tourists. Once feared as a threat, the fossa may lead the way toward improving the lives of both humans and animals in the no-longer-lost world of Madagascar.

Where did this new world come from? The island that is now Madagascar broke away from Africa and South America, which were connected 150 million years ago. Primitive plants and animals lived on the island. In the years that followed, early carnivores and other mammals may have drifted ashore on rafts of vegetation. The animals evolved in isolation until the recent past.

The family to which the fossa belongs is a unique line of carnivores that may pre-date modern wolves, cats, hyenas, bears, and other types of meat-eaters. Carnivores found throughout the rest of the world are not natives of Madagascar.

Humans first arrived in Madagascar about 2,000 years ago. These first explorers would have encountered 10-foot-tall flightless birds and lemurs as big as gorillas. Bones and other remains show that a large species of fossa also prowled the ancient forests of Madagascar. That

LOOK BOTH WAYS
Two young whooping crane siblings cross paths at the Aransas Wildlife Refuge in Texas.

Counting Cranes

BY JENNIFER S. HOLLAND

Adapted from "Counting Cranes," by Jennifer S. Holland, in *National Geographic*, June 2010

How many whooping cranes live in the wild? Not enough.
Multiple flocks once crisscrossed North America. Today
the number of cranes has fallen to a few hundred.

CRANE SPOTTING

Just above the treetops, a tiny red plane swoops in dizzying circles over Wood Buffalo National Park in Alberta, Canada. Pilot Jim Bredy banks hard for another pass. He and his two passengers try to spot familiar white smudges on the ground—adult whooping cranes with their young. This wilderness is the summer home of the last wild flock of Earth's most endangered crane.

The crane spotters include Bredy, Tom Stehn of the U.S. Fish and Wildlife Service, and Lea Craig-Moore of the Canadian Wildlife Service (CWS), and they're worried. The flock's population had reached 266 in the spring of 2008. But by the following spring, 57 had died, 23 of them on the birds' wintering grounds in south Texas. Drought had destroyed their main food—blue crabs and a plant called wolfberry.

Some cranes died during **migration**, often after striking power lines, the biggest known killer along the **flyway**. The high death count has added urgency to a new effort that tracks some migrating birds by attaching GPS units to their legs.

Whoopers, as the birds are called, are better off than they once were. In the mid-1800s their numbers plummeted as settlers turned wetlands into farms and hunted birds for food. When a major storm in 1940 led to the decline of a flock in Louisiana, only 22 wild whoopers remained.

Then, 42 years ago, a key event in the revival of the whooping crane took place. CWS biologist Ernie Kuyt went on a spring treasure hunt. A helicopter let him off on the soggy northern landscape, a vast expanse of meadow and ponds broken up by islands of spruce and willow trees. He trudged through muck that might have stolen his resolve. At the heart of a shallow pool, he spied a massive nest cradling a pair of blotchy eggs. Each was the size of an Idaho potato.

Kuyt tucked one egg into a wool sock, knowing that he was carrying home the possible salvation of a species. His excursion marked a major step in the effort to save the whooping crane. The egg in his sock helped seed a captive-breeding program that has been crucial to rescuing the cranes.

The whooping crane has become a symbol of endangered species, thanks in part to its fierce appeal. Standing nearly five feet tall, it dances with springing leaps and flaps of its mighty wings to win a mate. Beak to the sky, it fills the air with whooping cries.

The one remaining wild flock has slowly expanded. At the same time, conservationists have hatched and bred the birds in captivity and reintroduced them to their former habitat. These events have boosted the total number of cranes, including captive stock, to more than 500.

To rescue this darling among the world's 15 crane species, scientists first needed to answer a burning question: Where did whoopers nest and lay eggs in summer? Since the late 1890s biologists had known that the wild flock wintered on coastal marshland in south Texas. To crack the summer mystery, officials asked citizens to report sightings. Volunteers combed the migration route for clues.

Then, in the summer of 1954, a report came from a fire helicopter flying over a remote wetland 2,500 miles north of Texas, in northern Canada. By lucky chance, the flock had settled inside Wood Buffalo, the biggest national park in North America.

The park's remoteness has aided the cranes. Here whoopers face only natural predators such as wolves, bears, foxes, and egg-stealing ravens. They guard two-square-mile territories, build watery nests, and raise chicks on insect larvae, seeds, snails, and fish. "Wood Buffalo is and always will be truly wild," says Tom Stehn. "The birds are safe here."

MEAL TIME
A female whooper in Wood Buffalo National Park feeds her chick.

STILL AT RISK

The red plane dips to the west as Craig-Moore calls out another sighting. Even with information from past surveys, it will take multiple flights over several months, or 59 hours in the air, to finish one season's count: 62 nests, 52 chicks, and 22 fledglings, or young birds, spread over 100 square miles.

As of February 2010, the number of cranes in the wild sat at 263. They are holding steady, but they remain at great risk. In Texas, water diversion for farms and suburbs is boosting the salt content in coastal marshes, killing the crabs that cranes eat in winter. Lost wetlands, **oil sands** development in Canada, and wind power projects also mean fewer resting spots on the flyway. "It shows how fragile a success story this is," observes Stehn.

Today's population must expand at least fivefold before the crane is truly safe. Veterans of the effort believe that they can reach that goal. Says CWS biologist Brian Johns, "With enough habitat protection, in a couple of decades maybe the population won't need us anymore."

THINK ABOUT IT!

1 **Analyze Data** Which numbers in this article are most important, and what do they tell you about the situation the whooping crane faces?

2 **Synthesize** What makes the Wood Buffalo wilderness safe for the cranes?

BACKGROUND & VOCABULARY

flyway *n.* an established air route of migratory birds

migration *n.* (my-GRAY-shun) the regular movement of animals from one place to another for feeding or breeding

oil sands *n.* a deposit of loose sand or sandstone containing petroleum or other hydrocarbons

Last One

Adapted from "Last One," by Verlyn Klinkenborg,
in *National Geographic*, January 2009
Photographs by Joel Sartore

LONE FOX
This Catalina Island fox was bred in captivity as part of a program to help save the species.

In the United States as elsewhere, stopping the countdown to extinction means preserving healthy habitats. This is the aim of the Endangered Species Act.

WHO KILLED THE SPARROWS?

The final resting place of the last dusky seaside sparrow is a glass bottle in the Florida Museum of Natural History (photo above). The bird's eyes are heavily lidded. Its feathers have been ruffled by the alcohol that nearly fills the bottle. A paper tag states that the bird died on June 16, 1987.

Three and a half years after that sparrow's death, a brief entry appeared in the Federal Register, the publication that contains public notices from government agencies. It announced that the dusky seaside sparrow was now **extinct** and had been removed from the list of endangered and threatened wildlife. Neither the bird nor its critical habitat—the salt marshes of Florida's Merritt Island—would be protected any longer by the Endangered Species Act.

What killed the sparrows of Merritt Island? No one ate the dusky seaside sparrow or hunted it for sport. Its nests weren't destroyed. Nor was it killed off by a newly introduced predator. The sparrows were victims of human action.

For example, by spraying with the chemical DDT to control mosquitoes, humans altered the delicate **ecosystem** of the salt marshes. Humans hoped to improve their own lives by controlling pesky mosquitoes, but discovered, too late, that the seaside sparrow was finely attuned to its home in those salt marshes. That last bottled sparrow is how a species ends up when its habitat vanishes for good.

Red-cockaded woodpecker
12,210

Yellowfin madtom
5,800

Columbia Basin pygmy rabbit
0

How many are left?

The species featured on this page are endangered, near extinction, or extinct. The numbers in the photos indicate how many of each remain.

Delhi Sands flower-loving fly
1,000

Loggerhead sea turtle
90,000

Palos Verdes blue butterfly
4,300

BUGS AT RISK
The American burying beetle has
lost 90 percent of its original range.

22

SPECIES AND HABITATS

Ever since it was signed into law in December 1973, the Endangered Species Act has protected life forms at risk of disappearing. In a way it would be more accurate to call it the Endangered Species and Habitat Act, since the purpose of the law is to identify and then protect a species' critical habitat, whether it's an old-growth northern forest or an entire river.

The act has been **controversial** ever since it was signed. Why? Because it tries to save the habitats that plants and animals need to survive. Usually this means preventing humans from altering those ecosystems in any way. This is where the trouble arises.

What passed in 1973 was a lean, tough act. It called upon every department and agency in the federal government to work toward protecting endangered and threatened species. It required the federal government to cooperate with state governments. Futher, it pledged the United States would live up to international treaties whose purpose is to protect species facing extinction. It was, in a sense, a bill of rights for the rest of creation. In the beginning the act was inspired by an urgency and an increase in environmental awareness. Humans had suddenly realized that many species were disappearing in great numbers. This was an alarming trend.

THE ACT TODAY

Is the urgency any less today? In 1973 there were nearly 100 million fewer Americans and 2.8 billion fewer people lived on the planet. Scientists were just beginning to imagine how climate change might affect wildlife and plants. Today, report after report—on habitat loss, deforestation, the shrinking numbers of ocean fish, the drop in migratory bird populations—clearly shows that the picture for many species is far worse now than it was when the act became law.

Yet over time, the act has become a battleground, in part because it has created a conflict between the right to manage property and the need to protect the habitats critical to endangered species. There's no mistaking the intent of the act. It makes destroying critical habitats illegal, even on private land.

Some landowners believe that this part of the act violates their legal rights and they've taken their argument to the Supreme Court. Mostly they've lost. Some landowners have rushed ahead to develop their property while a species is being considered for listing. To prevent this, the federal government has created programs like Safe Harbor. Participating landowners agree to protect habitats. In exchange, the government agrees not to impose more limits on their property.

But the Endangered Species Act is itself endangered. It has not been given multiyear funding since the late 1980s. Instead it has survived with annual funds requested by the **Department of the Interior**. Also, fewer at-risk species are being brought under the act's protection. From 2000 to 2008 only 64 species were listed. In contrast, from 1988 to 1992 the total was 235.

Adding a species to the list is hard. First, a species has to be proposed, either by a government agency or a conservation group. Then candidates undergo scientific review and a public comment period. Opponents of the act have tried to make the act less effective, proposing changes that would allow federal agencies, not scientists, to decide whether to protect a species.

At present, 1,050 species in the United States and its surrounding waters are listed as endangered, at risk of extinction. Another 309 are listed as threatened, or likely to become endangered. Strategies for restoring shrinking populations exist for most of them. These measures include acquiring critical nesting beaches for sea turtles and restoring wetland habitat for the copperbelly water snake.

Critical habitat has been designated for only 520 species, however. When it comes to actual recovery, the numbers are not encouraging. Since 1973, only 39 U.S. species have been removed from the endangered and threatened list. Nine of those went extinct. Sixteen were removed when new evidence showed that a listed species was not, in fact, in danger. Only 14 have recovered enough to be removed from the list. Critics say those numbers show that the act is ineffective. But the numbers may instead show just how much opposition the act has faced. There are other ways to measure its success.

How many species might have vanished without the Endangered Species Act?

RARE BEAR
Between 1920 and 1940, only about 300 grizzly bears existed in the continental United States. Thanks to the Endangered Species Act, their numbers have improved. National Geographic photographer Joel Sartore photographed this grizzly and other species in this article for his Photo Ark project.

How many species might have vanished without the Endangered Species Act? Perhaps the best measure of the act's value is the very conflict it causes. It gives endangered species a day in court, and it helps us see the unintended consequences of our actions. It reminds us that what look like simple decisions—to build houses or plant more corn, for example—have to be considered within the context of nature. There, many lives are in the balance.

A TEST OF PRIORITIES

It's easy to see why we take the trouble to save creatures that are cultural icons. The bald eagle was removed from the list in 2007. Its numbers in the lower 48 states have been successfully restored from fewer than 500 nesting pairs in 1963 to about 10,000 pairs in 2007. The grizzly bear in Yellowstone National Park has graduated from the list. So have such impressive species as the peregrine falcon and the American alligator.

But what about the Delhi Sands flower-loving fly, an inch-long insect that now lives in only a few locations in southern California? Or the 165 remaining Salt Creek tiger beetles, which live in a few patches of salt marsh near Lincoln, Nebraska? What about Mississippi sandhill cranes, which are down to about 25 breeding pairs? Or the Higgins' eye pearly mussel, whose range has shrunk to a few pools in the Mississippi River and its tributaries? Most people have never heard of these creatures. They have no immediate appeal except their own beauty. They stand for nothing except their own way of life, which has been threatened by development, pollution, and the spread of invasive species.

The Endangered Species Act is really a test—and not just to see whether we can expend enough effort quickly enough to make a difference for the thousands of species at risk. The act is a test of **priorities**. After all the lessons we've learned about protecting species at risk, will the country recommit itself to the task? Will America return to the **idealism** of 1973?

Again and again, the battle over listing a species comes down to the choices we make in our everyday lives. Listing the greater sage grouse, for instance, would get in the way of natural gas and coal development in Wyoming. But we could offset those losses by conserving energy, something we ought to be doing anyway. Adding species to the endangered list takes the effort of scientists, lawmakers, conservationists, and ordinary citizens. What saves species, ultimately, is human restraint and the ability to balance our needs against the needs of other living beings on this planet.

We have no way of guessing how long human beings will survive, but one thing is certain. The better the chances of survival for plants, animals, and insects, the better our own chances will be.

THINK ABOUT IT!

1 **Identify Problems and Solutions** How can human behavior be changed to protect more animal species?

2 **Make Predictions** Do you believe the Endangered Species Act will be weakened in the future? Use details from the article and your own knowledge to make a prediction.

3 **Distinguish Fact and Opinion** Is the author of this article for or against the Endangered Species Act? Cite details from the article.

Right Whales

On the Brink, On the Rebound

BY DOUGLAS H. CHADWICK

Adapted from "Right Whales, On the Brink, On the Rebound,"
by Douglas H. Chadwick, in *National Geographic*, October 2008
Photographs by Brian Skerry

It's as huge as a sailing ship. It consumes 400,000 calories a day, surviving on prey a billionth of its size. This is the right whale. Could such amazing creatures ever become extinct?

IN THE NORTH ATLANTIC

They dive 600 feet, brushing their heads along the sea floor with raised patches of skin. Sometimes they swim upside down, big as sunken ships, warm-blooded and holding their breath in the cold and utter darkness. Then they open their huge jaws to let the currents sweep food straight in. This is one way North Atlantic right whales feed in the Bay of Fundy, on Canada's eastern coast. Or so the experts suspect, having watched the 40- to 80-ton animals surface with mud on their heads.

These animals got the name "right whale" from whalers who declared them the right, or best, whales to kill. Favoring shallow coastal waters, they passed close to ports, swam slowly, and often lingered on the surface. Such traits made them easy to **harpoon**. Once killed, they tended to conveniently float, thanks to their thick layer of blubber, or whale fat.

For centuries, the great whales of the North Atlantic were hunted **commercially**. They were prized for their oil and the strips of tough, flexible material called baleen harvested from the whales' mouths. In those days, baleen was used in women's fashions and in popular items such as umbrellas and whips. As a result of merciless hunting, all species of whales, including right whales, declined dramatically, with numbers falling by tens of thousands each year.

As the 20th century began, the number of right whales left was possibly in the low dozens. One of the greatest threats to the right whale population, commercial harpooning, wasn't banned until 1935.

HITTING BOTTOM
A southern right whale explores the ocean floor off the Auckland Islands of New Zealand.

CALVIN'S STORY

About 350 to 400 North Atlantic right whales exist today. These survivors migrate along North America's eastern coast, between feeding grounds in the Gulf of Maine and wintering sites farther south. Their route is roughly 1,400 miles one way, through an intensely urban stretch of ocean.

A research team from Boston's New England Aquarium spends the summer in Lubec, Maine, studying the whales that gather to feed off Nova Scotia's southern tip. The scientists have built a collection of around 390,000 photographs. Using these they can recognize nearly every whale in the population by the unique pattern of patches on its head, along with scars and other markings. Increasingly, the scientists are using DNA samples to identify individual whales.

One of their favorites is #2223, first seen in these waters in 1992. It was a baby and fond of diving playfully around boats. They named it Calvin. That same year a fisherman reported a **calf** circling its dying mother. When the team recovered the body of the female, they identified her as #1223—Delilah, Calvin's mom. Her body showed tissues crushed by a powerful collision, probably with a cargo ship. The eight-month-old calf's chance of survival looked grim. It should have been nursing Delilah's rich, warm milk for several more months.

In July 1993, researchers studying new photos from the bay found images that looked like a match for Calvin's baby pictures. Yes! The orphan had somehow made it alone. DNA from a skin sample taken in 1994 showed that curious, hardy Calvin was in fact a female whale.

The following year brought the first report of Calvin entering a surface-active group, or SAG, in which males and females mingle, splashing, shoving, and rolling playfully. Young whales of Calvin's age seem drawn to the excitement of SAGs where they get to practice adult mating behavior. Females of breeding age are the most valuable segment of the population, numbering fewer than a hundred. Calvin seemed on the verge of joining their ranks.

For three years, the researchers measured the young female's blubber thickness with ultrasound. It's a tricky operation. "One whale's reaction jolted the the boat hard enough to send me flying overboard," Amy Knowlton of the research team recalled. The researchers found Calvin growing plump, a good measure of whale health. On New Year's Eve in 1999, she was recorded for the first time in an expanse of shallow coastal waters off Georgia and Florida, where right whales go to give birth.

In the summer of 2000 Calvin was once again in the Bay of Fundy. This time she was snarled in fishing gear. Tough plastic ropes wrapped round her body, cut into her skin, and trailed behind her, slowing her down. Then researchers lost sight of the young female.

In a typical year, two to six right whales are found dead. At least half of them are killed by ship strikes or entanglement. Other animals simply disappear. More than three-quarters of North Atlantic right whales bear scars from encounters with fishing gear. How many of those missing are weighed down by ropes, nets, or crab and lobster pots for months or even years? As they starve and their fat reserves disappear, do they fight ever harder to reach the surface for each breath? Do they finally give in to pain and exhaustion and sink?

Months dragged by. Someone finally spotted Calvin in Cape Cod Bay during her journey back south. A disentanglement team raced for the site and made two attempts to slice away her bindings. They couldn't get them all, but when Calvin was seen in 2001, she had worked herself free of the remaining ropes.

Three years passed, and Calvin showed up occasionally. But she didn't show up in her usual summer haunts. Had being tangled in the ropes sent her into a downward spiral? At the end of December 2004, near the North Carolina coast, she presented herself—with a brand new calf. Seven months later, in 2005, they were in the Bay of Fundy, where Delilah had brought Calvin as an infant.

FARGO IN ACTION

The migration route traveled by North Atlantic right whales has grown ever more crowded with fishing activities and busy shipping lanes. Pollutants flow from river mouths. The underwater noise of ship traffic probably makes it increasingly difficult for the whales to

STRANGE BUT TRUE
The white patches on southern right whales' heads are called callosities and are large colonies of whale barnacles, parasitic worms, and whale lice.

communicate and keep track of one another. Though not as visible as wounds from propeller blades or fishing gear, heavy chemical and noise pollution may take a gradual toll.

During the 1980s the number of right whale babies born each year was around 12. The total fell sharply in the 1990s until just a single calf appeared in 2000. Since then, the average has risen to more than 20 calves a year. Yet this remains 30 percent below the whales' potential rate of reproduction. Why this low percentage? If scientists are to save the species, they need more data and more answers. Fast.

With today's technology, scientists can collect whale **dung** samples in the ocean and use intestinal cells from each sample to identify the individual that produced it. Researchers can also use the samples to tell the whale's general condition, its reproductive state, levels of stress, and presence of parasites.

COMEBACK STORY

Despite its low numbers, the North Atlantic right whale may not be the rarest of all the great whales. There may be no more than a few hundred North Pacific right whales. But on the other side of the equator, southern right whales have rebounded from a few hundred in the 19th century to at least 10,000. They offer a picture of what a safer future might be like for the other right whale species.

After feeding in the rich waters around Antarctica, the various groups of southern right whales migrate to wintering areas near Argentina, southern Africa, western and southern Australia, and New Zealand. The species has been increasing at a rate of up to seven percent a year. That's an impressive rate—close to the maximum possible for whales that can produce an offspring only every third year.

In July 2007, a team of scientists headed for the Auckland Islands, 300 miles south of New Zealand, to carry out **census** and DNA work. As the 82-foot sailboat slipped into a protected bay, only sunshine washed the deck. Soon, the native whales came out to investigate.

Curious southern right whales examined the boat for hours while penguins leaped along beside them. The whales' noisy breaths drowned out the sounds of waves, seabirds, and the young sea lions on shore. These whales were bigger than their relations the northern right whales. They bore no scars from collisions with boats or entanglements with nets.

Over the next three weeks, hundreds of southern right whales arrived. Researchers beat through the waves in a small boat to take identification photos and collect skin samples for study with small, hollow-tipped darts. One researcher observed, "We just saw more right whale calves in two hours than people will see all year in the whole North Atlantic."

MOTHER AND CHILD
A North Atlantic right whale
mother gets a playful bump from
her new calf in warm shallows
near Florida's Amelia Island.

> *"Whales are addictive. Once you see*
> *them, you don't want them to leave. Ever."*
>
> —DONNA MCCUTCHAN

WHALE SPOTTING

Protecting wildlife, even in the most remote places, gets harder all the time. Southern whales are doing fine for now. But keeping them that way will require better protection of wintering areas and migration routes. As fisheries and whale populations both expand, conflicts with whales can't be far off.

As for the whales of the North Atlantic, commercial fishing and sea transport are huge, important industries. Changing their operations along the entire eastern seaboard to protect a few hundred whales won't be easy or cheap.

Yet scientists say that saving just two mature females each year from being killed could change the trend for this endangered species. Instead of downward or level, the trend could be upward.

Put that way, the problem doesn't sound so hard to solve. At present, a network of air and water surveys and a force of volunteers keep a sharp eye out for right whales.

The volunteers include folks who gather for morning coffee and then drive from one overlook to the next. They also include residents who watch from the windows of their condos or who take elevators to the tops of the tallest buildings in order to catch a glimpse of these amazing whales.

When a surfacing whale is spotted from shore, roof, or sky, the information is quickly phoned in to the Early Warning System, which sends it to military and commercial ships. When operators of commercial ships over 300 gross tons enter right whale habitats, they must notify a Mandatory Ship Reporting System. This system automatically provides information about recent whale sightings.

It's far from a perfect system. Ship captains don't have to slow down if they don't feel like it. The federal government recently cut funding for right whale conservation research. Still, nothing seems to dampen the volunteers' enthusiasm.

Standing on a Florida beach, whale spotter Donna McCutchan said, "Most people in this development were like me. They had no idea whales winter here. Now everybody knows about them, and they know to call in if they spot one."

McCutchan herself hadn't seen a whale for weeks. She didn't mind waiting, she said. "I once got to watch a mother roll onto her back, and bottlenose dolphins started jumping over her. Whales are addictive. Once you see them, you don't want them to leave. Ever."

THINK ABOUT IT! ||||||||||||||||||||||||||||||||

1 **Draw Conclusions** The author says the right whales migrate through an "intensely urban" part of the Atlantic. What does he mean? Why is this an important piece of information?

2 **Compare and Contrast** Compare and contrast North Atlantic right whales with southern right whales.

BACKGROUND & VOCABULARY

calf *n.* the young of various large animals such as whales

census *n.* (SEHN-suhs) an official count

commercially *adv.* (kuh-MUR-shuh-lee) having to do with business; for profit

dung *n.* the solid waste produced by an animal's digestion; feces

harpoon *v.* (har-POON) to kill whales or large fish using a long, barbed spear

India's Grassland
KINGDOM

BY DOUGLAS H. CHADWICK

Adapted from "India's Grassland Kingdom," by Douglas H. Chadwick,
in *National Geographic*, August 2010

DANGER AFOOT
A charging rhino has the power and speed to destroy a jeep full of visitors to Kaziranga.

Each year about 70,000 Indian tourists and 4,000 foreign tourists visit Kaziranga National Park, India's "grassland kingdom." This subtropical parkland is home to 100 tigers, 2,000 one-horned rhinos, and 1,800 wild buffalo, among other species. Writer Douglas Chadwick explored Kaziranga's diversity.

THE ONE-HORNED RHINO

An Indian one-horned rhino—the kind that looks like it has shields bolted to its backside—weighs as much as an SUV. Once common throughout South Asia, this rhino species is represented today by fewer than 2,700 animals. A quarter live in ten little **reserves** in northern India and neighboring Nepal. Nearly all the rest—about 2,000 at the latest count—live in Kaziranga National Park. This 332-square-mile reserve has an average of 11 armored, irritable, one-horned rhinos per square mile.

A century ago, fewer than 200 of these rhinos were left in the north Indian state of Assam. Farming had taken over most of the fertile river valleys. Trophy hunters and poachers were destroying the survivors. Kaziranga was set aside in 1908 mainly to save the rhinos.

At first, Kaziranga held maybe a dozen rhinos, but the reserve was expanded over the years. It became a national park in 1974. During the late 1990s it grew again, this time doubling in size. Now Kaziranga is a premier rhino **sanctuary.** The park is the key to the one-horned rhino's future.

LIFE IN KAZIRANGA

Kaziranga National Park is a huge conservation success story. It is home to almost 1,300 wild elephants and 1,800 Asiatic wild water buffalo, the largest remaining population anywhere. Perhaps 9,000 hog deer, 800 swamp deer (a quickly vanishing species), scores of elk-like sambars, and hundreds of wild hogs also inhabit the reserve.

The park contains millions of pounds of prey, and one of the main consumers is the tiger. One day, as I watched a herd of deer, their raised tails tipped me off: tiger time. One had moved into the opening around a drying lake. But I couldn't find it. I was looking too low to the ground. The first thing I saw were legs. Then I was staring at a 500-pound, flame-colored cat looming over the tallest deer. Suddenly, the hunter and the hunted vanished. I was left to stare again into the sun-dappled stalks that had framed the magnificent tiger for just a moment.

The majority of India's tigers have disappeared in the last 25 years, victims of widespread deforestation, poaching, and weak protection at many reserves. Yet they seem to be thriving within Kaziranga. The official population estimate is now 90 to 100, which may be the largest per square mile in the world today.

How can the park support so many big animals in such a small area? The answer flows from a river. Beginning high in Tibet, the Brahmaputra River runs for 500 miles through India and Bangladesh. When torrential rains fall in summer, the river spills out over the valley. When the water recedes, it leaves behind a fresh layer of nutrient-charged silt. Tall grasses arise from the muck in vast fields of high-energy food.

We think of forests in the subtropics as the places with the most wildlife and the greatest

OUT FOR A MEAL
A group of elephants drinks and searches for food in Kaziranga.

need for conservation. But the habitats of the grassy floodplains have more large native animals and are far more rare. In addition to the fields of tall grasses reaching as high as 20 feet, Kaziranga has meadows of naturally short grasses. These open meadows are home to throngs of creatures.

On slightly higher ground, trees such as Indian lilac form airy forests roped with vines. Rhesus macaques—a species of monkey—troop past the trunks. Parakeets and great hornbills gracefully decorate the branches.

The grassy landscape is dotted with shallow lakes, which are recharged with water and fish by the floods. Migratory water birds crowd into Kaziranga's wetlands during the winter along with pelicans and storks. Rare fish-eagles scoop prey from ponds, and otters on the hunt sometimes arc from the water like dolphins. I even saw seven-foot-long Ganges River dolphins rising from the surface of the Brahmaputra.

Endangered in most places, these freshwater dolphins appear to be doing well along the park's length of the river, free from fishing pressures and entangling nets.

HUMANS AND RHINOS

Budheswar Konwar, my guide in Kaziranga, stopped our open-topped jeep so he could move an Indian tent turtle off a back road on a hot afternoon. The rest of us got out to stretch and watch. When I turned to check in the opposite direction, the view was terrible.

"Rhino!" It was close and churning toward us.

These tank-size creatures can sprint at more than 25 miles per hour. We didn't have time to leap into the vehicle and race away, so our guard fired a round. It was a perfectly placed shot. The bullet kicked up a stinging spray of dirt inches from the attacker's front foot. The rhino veered aside two seconds from us.

PERFECT CAMOUFLAGE
Amid the tall grass, a tiger's stripes become a cloak of invisibility.

Ten minutes later we were driving through forest along a raised dirt track when we saw a female rhino and two youths freshly emerged from a muddy wallow. The three ignored us.

We drove on, only to discover the mother rhino charging through the trees on a course aimed to collide with ours. Our guard couldn't even get off a shot before the female clobbered the jeep, which she far outweighed. His door caved in. The rhino was shoving us toward the road's edge and butting our jeep up onto two wheels.

Konwar had laid down a rule for Kaziranga: "No allowed for scared." I was breaking the rule while he gunned the engine, fighting for traction. At last the jeep leveled out and skidded free. But the rhino instantly gave chase, and it was still touch and go in a cloud of dust for several hundred feet.

Our destination was a site where the tracks of two tigers had been seen around a fresh rhino **carcass**. Tigers claim as many as 15 percent of the rhino calves in Kaziranga. This carcass spoke of tigers taking down an adult—a risky act.

The most serious threat to rhinos, though, still comes from humans, just as it did a century ago. That is why Kaziranga has nearly 600 guards, stationed between the unruly big animals and the poachers.

ELEPHANT GUIDES
Tourists riding elephants are safe from charging rhinos and well placed to observe the swamp deer of Kaziranga.

From 1985 through 2005, illegal hunters shot 447 Kaziranga rhinos and several guards. Guards killed 90 poachers and arrested 663. The number of rhinos poached annually dropped below nine starting in 1998. Then in 2007 it rose to 18. By the fifth week of 2008, when I arrived, five more had been killed.

A series of arrests followed, and the flurry of rhino poaching died down. Judging by past experience, though, more bad guys will show up sooner or later.

WILDLIFE PRESSURES

Kaziranga has another major problem, one that nobody can suppress. The park depends upon a large surrounding landscape to maintain its spectacular wildlife. In times of heavy flooding, wildlife flees the reserve for safety. It always has. Yet wherever the animals go these days, they encounter humankind.

You can get lost in the tall grass right up to Kaziranga's southern edge. Just beyond, however, you're among kids, dogs, chickens, milk goats, and miles of rice fields. A little farther on, you might reach a shed where a cow lies wounded by a tiger, while farmer Nijara Nath tells of discovering the tiger in the cattle pen.

On the park's north side, development creeps even closer. From high in a lookout tower, I could see only tame buffalo and cattle feeding across wetlands inside the park. The area experiences more elephant conflicts than almost any place in Assam, because it lies on a migratory route that elephant herds follow between Kaziranga and the Himalayan foothills to the north.

During high water, animals also migrate southward toward the southern hills. Five small but critical habitat bridges were recently added to the park. These are protected corridors along routes animals travel between reserves.

On the trip south, the animals confront National Highway 37, Assam's main east-west transportation route. Guards set up barriers to slow truck traffic at the most heavily used animal crossing sites. Nevertheless, elephants, rhinos, pythons, and deer on the move become road kill most every year.

Even if links to the southern hills are strengthened, what about the hills themselves? And what of the uplands sloping toward the Himalaya? Every year woodcutters, stone-quarry operators, and herders populate more of the state's forest reserves in those places, changing a continuous tree cover into a weedy patchwork of eroding slopes.

It helps that India has declared a Kaziranga elephant reserve that extends far to the south and a tiger reserve that reaches many miles north. At this stage, however, the reserves are little more than hopeful lines on a map, and the portions outside the national park keep filling with people hungry for land.

The challenge is to connect the remaining open land as much as possible. If the obstacles start to look overwhelming, think about the dedicated guards at lonely outposts. Think about Budheswar Konwar and the rhino-country rule. Remember? "No allowed for scared."

THINK ABOUT IT! ||||||||||||||||||||||||||||||

1 **Describe Geographic Information** Explain how a relatively small park can support such a rich variety of wildlife.

2 **Make Generalizations** What are two key steps that should be taken to preserve endangered populations of animals?

BACKGROUND & VOCABULARY

carcass *n.* (KAR-kuhs) a dead body, especially the body of a meat animal

reserve *n.* (rih-ZURV) a section of land legally set aside as an area where wildlife and their habitat are protected

sanctuary *n.* (SANK-chew-air-ee) a safe area for wildlife in which hunting is illegal

Document-Based Question

People from all walks of life are making efforts to protect endangered species. Scientists study the species and their habitats to learn as much as possible about them. Photographers and filmmakers share images of threatened species in the wild. Back home, people sign petitions, write to members of government, and raise money for environmental organizations. Each species removed from the endangered list is a victory for everyone.

DOCUMENT 1 Secondary Source

Big Cats Initiative

Scientists have sounded an alarm: Big cats may disappear from the wild in the next 20 years. In response, National Geographic launched the Big Cats Initiative in 2009. The excerpt below details how the initiative seeks to help humans and big cats coexist.

A major cause of big cat decline is retaliatory killing, which occurs when farmers and herders take revenge on big cats for attacking their livestock. [The Initiative is] working to promote coexistence between local [herders] and big cats by reducing the amount of human-wildlife conflict by:

- training local conflict officers
- building and improving protective livestock corrals
- using tourism to raise income and [help pay for] livestock losses
- placing tracking collars on big cats that work as a warning system for villagers
- using guard dogs to protect livestock
- relocating problem animals from conflict areas

from "Keeping the Peace," Big Cats Initiative, animals. nationalgeographic.com

CONSTRUCTED RESPONSE

1. Which activities do you think might be the easiest to implement? Which might be the most difficult? Give reasons for your answers.

DOCUMENT 2 Primary Source

Lion Lights

Night attacks by lions on cattle are a serious problem in the area of Kenya where Richard Turere tends his family's herd. Such attacks lead to the killing of critically endangered lions. Richard came up with a solution to this age-old lion versus human problem.

[Richard] observed that the lions never struck the homesteads when someone was awake and walking around with a flashlight. He concluded that lions equate torches with people so he took the bulbs from broken flashlights and rigged up an automated lighting system of four or five torch bulbs around the cattle stockade.

The bulbs are wired to an old car battery charged with a solar panel that operates the family television set. The lights flash in sequence giving the impression that someone is walking around the stockade.

In the two years that his lion light system has been operating, the Turere family has had no predation at night by lions. Richard's device costs less than ten dollars.

from "Lion Lights," by Stuart Pimm, newswatch. nationalgeographic.com, May 12, 2012

CONSTRUCTED RESPONSE

2. Do you think Richard's system will be widely adopted? Why or why not?

What are people doing to **protect** endangered species?

DOCUMENT 3 Primary Source
International Agreement

Wildlife activists demonstrate outside a meeting of the Convention on International Trade in Endangered Species (CITES) in 2013. CITES is an agreement between world governments that regulates trade in wildlife products. Its aim is to protect wild species from being hunted, fished, or harvested to extinction.

CONSTRUCTED RESPONSE

3. How are the protesters in the photo trying to help the endangered species?

Young activists protest the killing of endangered wildlife at the CITES meeting in Bangkok, Thailand, in March 2013.

PUT IT TOGETHER

Review Think about your responses to the Constructed Response questions and what you have learned from the articles in this book. Consider ways that humans are working to protect endangered species.

Synthesize Choose an endangered species featured in this book. Take notes on the species and what is happening to it. Then list actions being taken or that might be taken to protect the species.

Write What are people doing to protect endangered species? Write two paragraphs that describe what people are doing to protect the species you have chosen based on the notes you have taken.

INDEX

||||||||||||||||||||||||||||||||||||||||||||||||

SKILLS